Time to Fly!

Adapted by Andrea Posner-Sanchez
from the script "Horsefeathers" by Kent Redeker

Illustrated by Jason Fruchter

A GOLDEN BOOK • NEW YORK

randomhousekids.com
ISBN 978-0-7364-3362-4 (trade) — ISBN 978-0-7364-3363-1 (ebook)
Printed in the United States of America
10 9 8 7 6 5 4 3 2 1

One quiet morning, Uncle Bun is busy unloading supplies for his store when Peck, Toby, and Clementine come by.

"Howdy, Uncle Bun! Do you have any birdseed for me?" Peck asks.

"Sure do, Deputy. I've got everything from fishing poles to feather pillows," replies Uncle Bun as he tosses down a big bag of birdseed.

Clementine starts to gobble up the seeds.
"Birdseed is for birds!" Peck exclaims, taking
the bag away from Clementine. "You're not a bird.
You're a mule."

Uncle Bun offers Peck a better snack for his hungry mule. Peck reaches for an apple and accidentally knocks over the crate! He runs after the rolling fruit, yelling, "Stop, in the name of the law!"

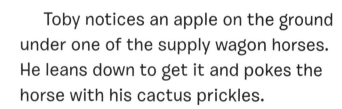

Toby notices an apple on the ground under one of the supply wagon horses. He leans down to get it and pokes the horse with his cactus prickles.

The poked horse is startled, and both horses rush off—with Uncle Bun still in the wagon!

A sack of flour flies off and lands on Peck's head. As the wagon zooms past Clementine, a barrel of molasses flies off and lands on *her* head. The mule manages to shake the barrel off, but now she is super sticky.

Sheriff Callie hears all the commotion and hurries out of the jailhouse. She jumps onto the back of the wagon and grabs the horses' reins.

"Whoa, fellers!" she cries.

The horses stop short—and Uncle Bun soars out of the wagon!

Sheriff Callie quickly lassoes Uncle Bun in midair. The pillow he was holding shoots out of his hands and bursts open . . .

. . . and feathers float down onto Clementine.

Peck and Toby rush over to Sheriff Callie and Uncle Bun. "What did we miss?" Peck asks.

"Nothing much," Uncle Bun says with a chuckle. "Sheriff Callie just saved the day again!"

The sheriff takes the horses to get some water. Uncle Bun heads to his store. And Toby and Peck pick up the apples to take to Clementine.

Toby notices Clementine first. He screams and drops his apples. "Clementine grew feathers!" he declares, pointing to the mule.

Peck looks puzzled for a moment, then says, "Clementine ate my birdseed. Maybe that's turning her into a bird. She'll be the world's first flying mule!"

They rush into Ella's Saloon and call everyone outside to see Clementine fly. The mule stands on top of a crate. Peck says, "Fly, girl, fly!"

But Clementine just steps down from the crate and eats an apple. The townspeople head back into the saloon, disappointed.

"It's not easy to fly!" Peck shouts to the crowd. "Clementine just needs some lessons."

Peck and Toby start Clementine's flying lessons right away.

"The first step is learning to jump," says Peck. He puts a broom on the ground and tells Clementine to jump over it.

She does—and gets a yummy apple as a treat.

Peck finds four springs for the next lesson. "These will help you jump even higher!" he says, attaching a spring to each of Clementine's hooves.

Clementine wobbles a bit as she gets used to the springs.

"Now jump!" Toby tells her.

The mule bounces high into the air. She bounces up and down the street. She even bounces on the roof of the jailhouse! Peck and Toby chase her, cheering.

"That was great bouncing, girl," Peck tells Clementine as he removes the springs. "Now you gotta get used to being up high."

Toby ties a bunch of balloons to Clementine's saddle. She rises into the air and floats away.

"Just look at her up there," says Toby. "She loves being a bird!"

Soon the knot holding the balloons comes undone, and one by one, the loose balloons drift away. Clementine manages to grab some balloon strings in her teeth, but there aren't enough left to keep her in the air. She begins to fall.

"Now's your time to fly, Clementine!" Peck shouts up to her. "Flap your wings!"

"Um, she hasn't grown wings yet," Toby points out.

Clementine lands on top of a moving train! She runs along the top of the train cars, all the way back to the caboose. Now there is nowhere for the scared mule to go—and the train is heading toward a tunnel!

"Uh-oh!" shouts Peck. "That tunnel will knock her off the train!"

"We've gotta save her!" cries Toby.

Before long, Sheriff Callie catches up with the train on her horse, Sparky. The sheriff twirls her noodle lasso and Clementine catches it with her teeth—just in time! The lasso springs back like a rubber band, causing Clementine to fly through the air.

Clementine lets go of the lasso and keeps on flying. She happily soars all the way back to town.

"She's flying! She's flying!" Peck cheers as he, Toby, and Sheriff Callie follow her.

But soon Clementine starts to fall. "She's falling! She's falling!" Peck cries.

"One soft landing, coming up!" says Sheriff Callie. She uses her lasso to pull a big haystack right under Clementine.

Peck is relieved to see that Clementine is okay.
"Now, would you mind telling me why you thought Clementine could fly?" Sheriff Callie asks.
"'Cause she grew feathers!" Toby explains.

The sheriff takes a closer look and plucks a feather off Clementine's head. She smiles. "These here feathers are just stuck on with molasses!" she tells them.

Peck gives Clementine another hug. "Aw, shucks. I guess we were so excited, we didn't think things through. Let's get you cleaned up and we'll go for a nice ride—one where you keep your hooves on the ground!"